I'M THE BOSS!

For Julia, Annabelle, and their big sister, Molly…
bosses one and all!

E.W.

Text copyright © 1994 by Elizabeth Winthrop
Illustrations copyright © 1994 by Mary Morgan
All rights reserved
Printed in the United States of America
First Edition

Library of Congress Cataloging-in-Publication Data
Winthrop, Elizabeth.
I'm the Boss! / Elizabeth Winthrop ; illustrated by Mary Morgan. —
— 1st ed.
p.   cm.
Summary: Tired of being told what to do by everyone else
in the family, Julia tries different ways of bossing them.
ISBN 0-8234-1113-3
[1. Family life — Fiction.]   I. Morgan, Mary, 1957–   ill.
II. Title.   III. Title: I am the boss!
PZ7.W768Iai   1994   93-9029   CIP   AC
[E] — dc20

I'M THE BOSS!

Elizabeth Winthrop

*illustrated by **Mary Morgan***

Holiday House/New York

Everybody bossed Julia around.

Her mother told Julia to eat her peas.

Her father told Julia to drink her milk.

Her older sister Molly told Julia to get out of her room.

Her baby sister Annabelle just said NO in a big loud voice
whenever Julia wanted to pick her up.
"Julia, leave Annabelle alone," said her father.

Even Marbles barked at Julia
and chewed on her slippers and jumped up on her legs.
Julia was not the boss of anything or anybody.
And she didn't like it.

"Mama, when do I get to be the boss?"
Julia asked her mother.
"When you're grown up," said her mother.

One day, Julia dressed up in her mother's high heels
and her big flouncy dress and her wide-brimmed hat.

She picked up her mother's briefcase
and marched around the house.
Now she was all grown up.

She made lists of things to do
and talked on the phone to many very important people.
She pointed her pencil at her baby sister Annabelle.
"I'm the boss," she said.
"You have to do what I say."
Annabelle stuck her thumb in her mouth and stared at Julia.
"It's time to take your thumb out of your mouth," said Julia.
Annabelle went on sucking and staring.

Julia knocked on Molly's door.

"Molly," she said. "Open up. This is the boss."

Molly opened the door and looked at her.

"I have on my big boss clothes.

Now it's time to clean up your room," said Julia.

"Who says?" Molly asked.

"Me," said Julia. "I'm the boss."

"Mama's the boss," said Molly. She closed the door.

"But I'm wearing the boss clothes," Julia cried.

"Now open this door."

But Molly didn't.

Julia took all the boss clothes off
and waited for her father to get home from work.
"Daddy, how do I get to be the boss?" Julia asked.
"Well, my boss has a big sign on his door and
he shouts a lot," Daddy said with a laugh.

Julia went back to her room.
She drew a picture of a big, mean, bossy-looking person
and hung it around her neck.

Then she marched around the house,
blowing her horn and shouting,
"Here comes the boss. Everybody watch out."

Molly peeked out from behind her door.
"Time to set the table, Molly," Julia shouted
and blew on her horn.

Molly stuck her fingers in her ears.

Marbles howled.

Annabelle crawled out from under the table.

"No more dirty diapers, Annabelle," Julia shouted.

"I'm the boss. Time to use the potty."

Annabelle burst into tears.

"JULIA," cried her mother.

"What is going on here?"

"I'm the boss, Mama," explained Julia.

"See my boss sign."

"Signs and loud noises don't make you the boss,"
  said her mother.
  Julia stamped her foot.
"Well, how do I get to be the boss?"
  she asked.
  Her mother sat down and thought.
"I know," she said.
"I'm the Big Boss and
  you're the Little Boss."
  She made Julia a special hat
  that said LITTLE BOSS.

Julia put on her hat
and marched down the hall.
When Molly saw it,
she pulled it off,
and Annabelle just giggled.

Marbles picked up the hat and chewed on it.

"Marbles, stop that!" Julia said
in her loud bossy voice.

Marbles looked up.

"No more chewing," said Julia.

Marbles opened her mouth.

The hat fell out.

"Good dog," said Julia.

Marbles wagged her tail.

"Now I'm the boss of you," said Julia.

"You have to sit."

Marbles kept on wagging her tail.

"SIT," Julia said again.

She pushed down on Marbles's bottom.

Marbles sat.

"Good dog," Julia said again.

Marbles jumped up on Julia.

"NO," said Julia. "DOWN!

No more jumping."

Marbles wagged her tail some more.

Julia put on her hat.

"Remember, I'm the boss, Marbles.

You have to listen to me."

Marbles barked.

"Now we are going for a walk."

Marbles barked again.

So Julia put on Marbles's leash

and took her for a walk around the house.

"Heel," said Julia.

"Sit," said Julia.

"Down," said Julia.

Julia was such a good boss that sometimes Marbles heeled

and sometimes she sat and . . .

sometimes she even lay down
and stayed there.

And when she did that
Julia lay right down beside her
and hugged her,
because finally . . .
she was the boss
of *somebody*.